CW00694914

THE UNEXPURGATED ADVENTURES OF

SHERLOCK HOLMES

BOOK 2

THE MYSTERIOUS CASE OF MR. GINGERNUTS

by NP Sercombe

The un-edited manuscript originally entitled *The Red-Headed League* written by Dr. John Watson and Sir Arthur Conan Doyle

Illustrations by Emily Snape

This novel is entirely a work of fiction. The names, characters and incidents portrayed in it are the work of the author's and illustrator's imaginations. Any resemblance to actual persons, living or dead, events or localities, is entirely coincidental.

Published by EVA BOOKS 2019 – c/o Harry King Films Limited
1&2 The Barn
West Stoke Road
Lavant
n/r Chichester
West Sussex PO18 9AA

A CIP catalogue record for this book is available from the British Library.

ISBN 978-1-9996961-1-5 (Hardback)

Book layout & Cover design by Clare Brayshaw.

Cover illustration by Emily Snape.

Set in Bruce Old Style.

Prepared and printed by: York Publishing Services Ltd
64 Hallfield Road, Layerthorpe, York YO31 7ZQ

Tel: 01904 431213

Website: www.yps-publishing.co.uk

THE UNEXPURGATED ADVENTURES OF

SHERLOCK HOLMES

Books in the Series:

A BALLS-UP IN BOHEMIA
THE MYSTERIOUS CASE OF MR. GINGERNUTS
THE CASE OF THE RANDY STEPFATHER
MY FIRST PROPER RURAL MURDER
THE ORANGES OF DEATH!

Nicholas Sercombe is a writer and producer for film and television. He has been lucky enough to work in comedy for most of the Holocene period with some of the greatest performers and writers. He is most comfortable when reading Conan Doyle and even happier when re-writing these extraordinarily entertaining stories by Dr. John Watson.

Emily Snape is a coffee addicted, London based illustrator, who's work can be found internationally on books, magazines, the web, television and even on buses.

She studied at Central Saint Martins, Bristol and Kingston and is rarely found without a pencil in her hand. She loves sketching in the streets of London and thinks life is too short for matching socks.

For ginger-haired people who enjoy laughing

The Mysterious Case of Mr. Gingernuts

(*published in The Strand as* THE RED-HEADED LEAGUE by Dr. Watson and Arthur Conan Doyle)

One day in the autumn of last year, I had returned to 221B Baker Street from my day's surgery in Kensington of just a single patient consultation, who turned out to be a healthy hypochondriac. I was weary and wished to put my feet up in front of the fireplace but when I opened the door, I found my friend, Mr. Sherlock Holmes, in deep conversation with a very stout, florid-faced, elderly gentleman, with fiery red hair. One look was all I needed! I spun on my heel and headed for the safety of Baker Street, when Holmes pulled me up abruptly back into the room and closed the door behind me.

'You could not have come at a better time, my dear friend' he said cordially.

I stole another look into the room and relaxed. 'Sorry, Holmes! For a moment then I thought it was Professor Moriarty sitting there.'

'Don't be ridiculous, Watson. You have never met the Professor. And since when was the Professor a ginger tom?'

'My apologies, Holmes. He must be a prospective client? And what orange hair he has! Do you still want me to stay?'

Holmes locked the door and swept his arm out towards the room.

'My dear Doctor, you hardly need an invitation to enter your own residence. Come along, I'll introduce you....Mr. Wilson, this gentleman has been my partner and...No, Mr. Wilson, my business partner. He has also been my helper in many of my most successful cases and I am sure he will be of the utmost use to me in yours.'

The stout gentleman half rose from his chair and gave me a bob of greeting, having dispelled the lurid smirk from his small fat-encircled eyes when he thought that Holmes and I polished the fireman's helmet together. The truth is that after the annulment of my marriage I was, once again, Adam seeking Eve in the Garden of Eden and, as Holmes once declared immodestly, he was "Hermes, the Argus-slayer, in constant pursuit of Aphrodite!" But the number of lewd thoughts that go through peoples' minds just because the two of us lived together in the same apartment were legion around town. This was due to people like this Mr. Gingernuts, who encouraged the seeds of unwelcome gossip to spread on the ill wind of malevolent rumour.

'Try the sofa' said Holmes, relapsing into his armchair, and putting his fingertips together, as was his custom when in judicial moods or, more likely, when he was about to embark upon a subtle excavation of a blocked nostril with his pinkie. 'I know, my dear Watson, that you share my love of all that is bizarre and outside the conventions and humdrum of everyday life...'

'Please, Holmes, you promised not to say anything!'

'...MY POINT being that it is this curiosity of yours that has prompted you to start to chronicle, and, if you will excuse me saying so, to *embellish* my own little adventures.'

'Your cases have indeed been of the greatest interest to me and the only embellishment is a little added colour where absolutely necessary,' I replied. My goodness yes! These adventures with Sherlock Holmes had been of enormous interest to me. Recently, *The Strand* magazine had published my first adventure, *A Balls-up In Bohemia* – under the title of *A Scandal In Bohemia* – and it had become an overnight success, quite the talking-point in the drawing rooms and clubs around town. Regular features for serialisation had been ordered by the editor, Mr. Newnes. Future chronicles had the potential to make me a tidy fortune, way in excess possibly of any I may have as a doctor in general practice.

'You will remember that I remarked the other day, just before we went into the very simple problem presented by Miss Mary Sutherland, that for strange effects and extraordinary combinations we must go to the life itself, which is always far more daring than any effort of the imagination.'

'A proposition that I took the liberty of doubting.'

'You did, Doctor, but none the less you came around to my point of view, for otherwise I shall keep on piling fact upon fact on you until your reason breaks down under them and acknowledges me to be right.'

He just had to rub my nose in it! 'Yes, Holmes, I admit, you were right, and I was wrong.'

'Now Mr. Jabez Wilson here has been good enough to call upon me this morning, and to begin a narrative which promises to be one of the most singular which I have listened to for some time. You have heard me remark that the strangest and most unique things are very often connected not with the larger but with the smaller crimes, and occasionally, indeed, where there is room for doubt whether any positive crime has been committed. Perhaps, Mr. Wilson, you would have the great kindness to recommence your narrative. MR. WILSON!'

Mr. Wilson had nodded off. I thought that I should help the poor fellow, who was clearly bored out of his mind listening to Holmes and me drone about our previous exploits. I stood up, shook Mr. Wilson's shoulder until he had awoken and walked over to one of the windows.

'I'll open this a little, Holmes. It is a trifle warm in here.'

'Please pay attention Mr. Wilson! I ask you, not merely because my friend Dr. Watson has not heard the opening part, but also because the peculiar nature of the story makes me anxious to have every possible detail from your lips. As a rule, when I have heard some slight indication of the course of events, I am able to guide myself by the thousands of other similar cases which occur to my memory. In the present instance I am forced to admit that the facts are, to my best belief, unique.'

The detective's outburst had jarred our portly client and he puffed out his chest with an appearance of some little pride and pulled a dirty and wrinkled newspaper from the inside pocket of his greatcoat. As he glanced down the advertisement column, with his head thrust forward, and the paper flattened out upon his knee, I took a good look at the man, and endeavoured after the fashion of my companion to read the indications that might be presented by his dress or appearance.

I did not gain very much, however, by my inspection. Our visitor bore every mark of being an average commonplace British tradesman: obese, pompous and slow. He wore baggy grey shepherd's check trousers, a not overclean black frock coat, unbuttoned in the front, and a drab waistcoat with a heavy brassy Albert chain, and a square pierced bit of metal dangling down as an ornament. A frayed top hat and a faded brown overcoat with a wrinkled velvet collar lay upon a chair beside him. Altogether, look as I would, there was nothing remarkable about the man save his blazing red head, and the expression of extreme chagrin and discontent upon his features.

Sherlock Holmes's quick eye took in my occupation, and he shook his head with a smile as he noticed my questioning glances. 'Beyond the obvious facts that he has at some time done manual labour, that he takes snuff, that he is a Freemason, that he has been in China, that he has done a considerable amount of writing lately and has a hole through the side of his John Thomas, I can deduce nothing else.'

Mr. Jabez Wilson jumped up from his chair, his right hand clasping the paper, but his eyes fixed intently upon my companion.

'How in the name of good fortune did you know all that, Mr. Holmes?' he asked, slowly descending back into his seat. 'How did you know, for example, that I did manual labour. It is as true as gospel, for I began as a ship's carpenter.'

'Your hands, my dear sir. Your right hand is much larger than your left. You have worked with it, and the muscles are more developed.'

I'll leave you, dear reader, to decide if this is the only possible reason for the larger mitt, especially if he had spent so much time at sea. Looking at the man as a physician, I was able to make one diagnosis right now: that Mr. Jabez Wilson had simply not had the company of the fairer sex for a very long period of time at a crucial moment in his life.

'Well, the snuff, then, and the Freemasonry?'

'You have an inflamed left nostril. And I won't insult your intelligence by telling you how I read the latter, especially as, rather against the strict rules of your order, you use an arc and compass breastpin.'

'Ah, of course, I forgot that. But the writing?'

'What else can be indicated by that right cuff so very shiny for five inches, and the left one with the smooth patch near the elbow where you rest it upon the desk.'

'Well, maybe, but China?'

'The fish which you have tattooed immediately above your right wrist could only have been done in China. I have made a small study of tattoo marks and have even contributed to the literature of the subject. That trick of staining the fishes' scales of a delicate pink is quite peculiar to China.'

'All very well but the very notion, Mr. Holmes, that you can see through the fabric of my fine worsted trousers and view my John Thomas is absolutely preposterous!'

'I have no need to have such specialist vision. That ornament hanging from your chain I believe to be known as a 'Prince Albert,' hence my final conclusion that if it hangs from your waistcoat and *capitibus meridianam* it is attached not to a watch, *ipso facto,*

I surmise it is attached to your male appendage and that the present state of your undercarriage is one of ventilation of a single drilled hole in its shaft. Am I not correct, Mr Wilson?'

Mr. Jabez Wilson laughed heavily. 'You most certainly are, Mr. Holmes! Well I never!' said he. 'I thought at first that you had done something clever, but I see that there was nothing in it after all.'

'It's easy when you know how, Mr. Wilson.' And then Holmes leaned towards me, in quite a state of piquant agitation. 'I begin to think, Watson, that our friend here is a bit of a smart-alec. *'Omne ignotum pro magnifico.''*

'What do you mean? My dear friend, I have no grounding in the classics.'

Holmes tapped the side of his nose with his long forefinger and then pointed it straight at my pituitary gland.

'Yes, yes, yes... I have the gist of what you are getting at, Holmes. He's not the first, and nor will he be the last fool to think your methods facile. Let's hear what he has to say for himself and, if his problem is not entertaining enough for our tastes, we can tear off those 'fine worsted trousers,' paint his bum blue and throw him out onto the pavement!'

Holmes managed a wan smile of agreement to my proposal and turned his attention back to Mr. Gingernuts. 'Can you not find the advertisement, Mr. Wilson?'

'Yes, I have got it now,' he answered, with his thick, red finger planted half-way down the column. 'Here it is. This is what began it all. You just read it for yourself, sir.'

I took the paper from him, and read as follows: -

"TO THE RED-HEADED LEAGUE. On account of the bequest of the late Ezekiah Hopkins, of Lebanon, Penn, USA., there is now another vacancy open which entitles a member of the League to a salary of four pounds a week for purely nominal services. All red-headed men who are sound in body and mind, and above the age of twenty-one years, are eligible. Apply in person on Monday, at eleven o'clock, to Mr. Sidney Goodtime, at the offices of the League, The City Lido, Pope's-Court, Fleet Street."

'What on earth does this mean?' I ejaculated, after I had twice read over the extraordinary announcement.

Holmes chuckled, and wriggled in his chair, as if he was following my lead. 'It is a little off the beaten track, isn't it?' said he. 'And now, Mr. Wilson, off you go from scratch, and tell us about yourself, your household, and the effect which this advertisement had upon your fortunes. You will make a note, Doctor, of the paper and the date.'

'It is *The Morning Chronicle*, of April 27, 1890. Just four months ago.'

'Very good. Now, Mr. Wilson?'

'Well, it is just as I have been telling you, Mr. Sherlock Holmes,' said Jabez Wilson, mopping his forehead. 'I have a small pawnbroker's business at Coburg Square near the City.'

It all made sense to me now. Ezekiah this, Jabez that. Pawnbroking. Coburg Square. I knew what we were dealing with all right. Whilst Mr. Wilson continued with his oration I leant over to my companion.

'Psst! Holmes! You do realise we are dealing with a four-wheeler?

'This puzzle is of the most extraordinary interest to me, Watson. I care not for the race or creed who engages my services.'

'Yes, but that's exactly my point. You are offering a service, which by definition means payment for your time and expertise, and you can bet your last farthing there won't be a penny in it for us from one of his lot.'

'Sssh, you anti-Semite, you! You are missing valuable information. Sharpen your pencil!'

'I shall, but don't forget we need money, even to pay the rent. We are two months in arrears.' And then I grasped a pencil from my top pocket and adapted an unopened letter from the Azerbaijani prayer mantel into a notepad.

'Business has been slow recently,' said Mr. Wilson. 'I used to be able to keep two assistants, but now I keep only one; and I would have a job to pay him, but that he is willing to come for half wages, so as to learn the business.'

'Oh,here it comes!' I whispered. 'Our Shylock is warming up nicely to the task of informing us, eventually, of his impecuniosity.'

Holmes ignored my commentary. 'What is the name of this obliging youth?' asked Sherlock Holmes to Mr. Wilson.

'His name is Vincent Spaulding, and he's not such a youth either. It's hard to say his age. I should not wish a smarter assistant, Mr. Holmes; and I know very well that he could better himself and earn twice what I am able to give him. But after all, if he is satisfied, why should I put ideas into his head?'

'Why indeed? You seem most fortunate in having an *employé* who comes under the full market price and is of any practical use, or doesn't interrupt your professional actions with crass and stupid remarks' he said, his eyes flicking directly over to me, registering my piqued reaction, then turning his head away from our guest and blowing me a silent kiss. The cheek of it! He turned back to Mr. Wilson. 'I don't know that your assistant is not as remarkable as your advertisement.'

'Oh, just like your fellow here, he has his faults too,' said Mr. Wilson, and Holmes nodded sagely, supporting more witty assassination of my character. 'Never was such a fellow for photography. Snapping away with a camera when he ought to be improving his mind...'

'Hear hear!' interjected Holmes.

'...and then diving down into the cellar like a rabbit into its hole to develop the pictures. That is his main fault; but on the whole, he's a good worker. There's no vice in him.'

'He is still with you, I presume?'

'Yes, sir. He and a girl of fourteen, who does a bit of simple cooking, and keeps the place clean – that's all I have in the house, for I am a widower of some years now, and never had any family. We live very quietly, sir, the three of us; and we keep a roof over our heads, and pay our debts, if we do nothing more. The first thing that put us out was that advertisement. Spaulding, he came down into the office just this day eight weeks ago with this very paper in his hand, and he says:

'I wish to the Lord, Mr. Wilson, that I was a red-headed man.'

'Why is that?' I ask.

'Why,' says he, 'here's another vacancy on the League of the Red-headed men. It's worth quite a little fortune to any man who gets it, and I understand that there are more vacancies than there are men, so that the trustees are at their wits' end what to do with the money. If my hair would only change colour, here's a nice little crib already for me to step into.'

'Why, what is it then?' I asked. 'You see, Mr. Holmes, I am a very stay-at-home man, and, as my business came to me instead of my having to go at it, I was often weeks on end without putting my foot over the door-mat. In that way I didn't know much of what was going on outside, and I was always glad of a bit of news.'

'Have you never heard of the League of Red-headed Men?' he asked, with eyes open.

'Never!'

'Why, I wonder at that, for you are eligible yourself for one of the vacancies.'

'And what are they worth?' I asked. Well, that would be his first question, dear reader, would it not? How much? Is that all? Ish! I wouldn't get out bed for twice that!

'Oh, merely a couple of hundred a year, but the work is slight, and it need not interfere very much with one's other occupations.'

'Well, Mr. Holmes, you can easily think that that made me prick up my ears, for the pawnbroking business has not been over good for some years, and an extra couple of hundred would have been very handy.'

'Tell me about it!' said I. 'You should spend some time around here, Mr. Wilson, and see if you fall head-first over any piles of cash. Even wearing a blindfold, it would be, dear sir, an impossibility!'

'Oh, you are such a bore, Doctor!' exclaimed Holmes. 'I apologise, Mr. Wilson. My companion can think of nothing but money; I fear that, at times, he should have been a money lender. Oh! My apologies, that is what you do Mr. Wilson. Pray, continue with your most fascinating story.'

'Well,' said he, showing me the advertisement, 'you can see for yourself that the League has a vacancy, and there is the address where you should apply for particulars. As far as I can make out, the League was founded by an American millionaire, Ezekiah Hopkins, who was very peculiar in his ways. He was himself red-headed, and he had a great sympathy for all red-headed men; so, when he died, it was found that he had left his enormous fortune in the hands of trustees, with instructions to apply the interest to the providing of easy berths to me whose hair is of that colour. From all I hear it is splendid pay, and very little to do.'

'But' said I, 'there would be millions of red-headed men who would apply.'

'Not so many as you might think,' he answered. 'You see it is really confined to Londoners, and to grown men. This American had started from London when he was young, and he wanted to do the old town a good turn. Then, again, I have heard it is no use your applying if your hair is light red, or dark red, or anything but real, bright, blazing, fiery red. Now, if you cared to apply, Mr. Wilson, you would just walk in; but perhaps it would hardly be worth your while to put yourself out of the way for the sake of a few hundred pounds.'

'Now, it is a fact, gentlemen, as you may see for yourselves, that my hair is of a very full and rich tint, so that it seemed to me that, if there was to be any competition in the matter, I stood as good a chance as any man that I had ever met. And I could, of course, prove it was genuine.'

'Really? And just how did you do that, Mr. Wilson?' asked Holmes.

To my horror, Mr Jabez Wilson stood up in front of us and commenced the unbuttoning of his fly. 'See!' he cried, and then dropped his check trousers to reveal his outstanding masculinity nesting in a raging tangle of bright orange hair.

'THAT WILL NOT BE NECESSARY!' shouted Holmes, and we both swung our heads away. We heaved a sigh of relief as our speaker's hands moved up and restored the garish trousers back into position. He sat back down in his chair. As he continued upon his discourse, Holmes shot me a look of mock terror behind Wilson's back – a moment of true silliness – and I tried my best to choke back laughter.

'Vincent Spaulding seemed to know so much about it that I thought he might prove useful, so I just ordered him to put up the shutters for the day, and to come right away with me. He was very willing to have a holiday, so we shut the business up, and started off for the address that was given us in the advertisement.

'I hope never to see such a sight as that again, Mr Holmes. From north, south, east and west every man who had a shade of red in his hair tramped into the City to answer the advertisement. Fleet Street was choked with red-headed folk, and Pope's Court looked like a coster's orange barrow. I should not have thought there were so many in the whole country as were brought together by that single advertisement. Every

Mr. Wilson proved he was a true red-head.
It turns out he was also Jewish.

shade of colour they were – straw, lemon, orange, brick, Irish Setter, liver, clay and, inevitably, carrot; but as Spaulding said, there were not many who had the real vivid flame-coloured tint. When I saw how many were waiting, I would have given it up in despair; but Spaulding would not hear of it. How he did it I could not imagine, but he pushed and pulled and battled until he got me through the crowd, and right up to the steps which led to the office. There was a double stream upon the stair, some going up in hope, and some coming back dejected; but we wedged in as well as we could, and soon found ourselves in the office.'

'Your experience has been a most entertaining one,' remarked Holmes, who suddenly sat bolt upright in his armchair as his client paused, pulled out a tin of white powder and refreshed his memory with a huge pinch of snuff. When he had shot a load up each nostril, the great detective became more anxious. 'Pray continue your very interesting statement, and, if you want my help in this matter, don't hog the Colombian.'

Holmes scooped himself a generous spoonful of powder and remarked: 'From Cartagena. Excellent! Thank you, Mr. Wilson.' I was impressed but it never failed to amaze me how my friend's olfactory system could sniff out certain varieties of snuff so accurately, accompanied indeed by his profound knowledge of its various geographical origins. Mr. Wilson approached his task with renewed vigour.

'There was nothing in the office but a couple of wooden chairs and a deal table, behind which sat a friendly looking man with absolutely no hair whatsoever. I could only assume this was the man known as Sidney Goodtime. He said a few words to each candidate as he came up, and then he always managed to find some fault in them, which would disqualify them. Getting a vacancy did not seem to be such a very easy matter after all. However, when our turn came up, Mr. Goodtime was much more favourable to me that to any of the others, and he closed the door as we entered, so that he might have a private word with us.'

'This is Mr.Jabez Wilson,' said my assistant, 'and he is willing to fill a vacancy in the League.'

'And he is admirably suited for it,' the other answered. 'He has every requirement. I cannot recall when I have seen anything so fine.' He took a step backwards, cocked his head on one side, and gazed at my hair until I felt quite bashful. In fact, I thought it was time to do something to distract him, and so I tried to break the ice, so to speak.

'Tell me, Mr. Goodtime, what happened to your own hair?'

'Well, he suddenly plunged forward, wrung my hand, and cried 'Alopecia!' to which I replied, 'Bless you!' but please would he kindly answer my enquiry?'

'I didn't sneeze, you fool! I suffer from al-o-pe-c-i-a, the hair-loss malady. I am about to offer you the position with the League, and I would have hoped for better manners in the first place. Nevertheless, I hope you will excuse me for taking an obvious precaution.' With that he seized my hair in both his hands and tugged until I yelled with the pain. 'There is water in your eyes,' said he, as he released me. 'I perceive that all is as it should be...'

'Thank goodness for that!' I cried, but before I could count my chickens he continued with '...but we have to be careful, for we have twice been deceived by wigs and once by paint. I must therefore ask you to make one small sacrifice to secure your position.'

Holmes looked over at me, wearing one of the biggest smirks of the meeting, as he tried desperately to control his laughter. I had to tear myself away from his direction as I started to feel my own convulsions on the inside. Mr. Wilson kept going, regardless of our condition.

'And, although I was, at first, somewhat embarrassed to stand on the window sill overlooking Fleet Street, naked as the day I was born, it enabled Mr. Goodtime to lend credibility to the fact that the League had secured the right man for the job, and it had the added effect of causing the unsuccessful candidates to disperse at the greatest speed possible, some screaming in mock horror at my nakedness but most laughing hysterically at my good fortune. Mr. Goodtime himself had to wipe some tears from his own eyes as he led me back into the room and sat down at his desk in a state of jubilation. He even remarked to his secretary: 'that was the best one yet!' Then, he entertained us with some fond memories. "I could tell you some funny tales, the best being the chancer with the cobblers' wax, but it would probably disgust you to learn such a state of depraved humanity."'

Holmes leaned forwards in his chair and let out a stifled whimper. I took just one glance at him, that look that close friends or companions can convey thoughts by the slightest of facial expressions, and I knew that he was losing his self-control.

'My name is Sidney Goodtime,' said Wilson, continuing his story 'and I am myself one of the pensioners upon the fund left by our noble benefactor. Are you a married man, Mr. Wilson? Have you a family?'

I answered that I had not. His face fell immediately.

'Dear me!' he said gravely, 'that is very serious indeed! I am sorry to hear you say that. Are you one of *those*, then? A whoopsie? A fairy? One of the *Bourneville brigade*?'

Well, for Holmes it was one metaphor too many. 'Bourneville brigade?' he exclaimed as he collapsed into a fit of uncontrollable laughter. It wasn't his fault because even I just couldn't believe the naked honesty with which this description had been made by Mr. Wilson.

'I am most certainly not Mr. Holmes!' shouted our temporary guest. 'And that is precisely what I said to Mr. Goodtime!' Mr. Wilson looked on with despair at Holmes doubled-up and rolling around in his chair. 'Please stop it, Mr. Holmes! Give me some time to reason.' But Holmes was corpsing; I think that the "snuff" he had piped aboard earlier was now taking control of his autonomic functions.

'Oh, never mind; I'll carry on with my story...' 'Good!' said Mr. Goodtime. 'The fund was, of course, for the propagation of and spread of the red-heads as well as for their maintenance. It is exceedingly unfortunate that you should be a bachelor.'

'My face lengthened at this, Mr. Holmes, for I thought that I was not to have the vacancy after all; but, after thinking it over a for a few minutes, he said it would be all right.'

'We must stretch a point in favour of a man with such a head of hair as yours. And I suppose we might be able to set up a love match with one of the League's female associates. Yes, that will be it!'

Mr. Goodtime asked impertinent questions about Mr. Wilson's marriage propects.

I leaned into my friend's ear. 'They supply women for free! Surely this mystery is worthy of further investigation?' I noticed Mr. Wilson leaning forwards tetchily, trying to earwig my words.

Holmes swivelled his head towards me and hissed 'Hold on to your libido, Watson! I have yet to decide whether this dull ginger man is a client in our midst.' He looked up. 'Pray, continue Mr. Wilson.'

Mr. Wilson sighed and settled himself down once again. 'When shall you be able to enter upon your new duties?' Mr. Goodtime enquired of me.

'Well, it is a little awkward, for I have a business already,' said I.

'You don't make it easy for me, do you Mr. Wilson!' And he threw a glance at Spaulding.

'Oh, never mind about that!' said Vincent Spaulding. 'I shall be able to look after that for you.'

'What would be the hours?' I asked.

'Ten till two' said Mr. Goodtime.

'Now a pawnbroker's business is mostly done of an evening, Mr Holmes, especially Thursdays and Fridays, which is just before pay-day...'

As if we needed to be taught the finer nuances of the pawnbroking business! His voice faded away as I cast my mind back to the many occasions, I had been arguing the market value of our silver plate with the local Shylock when we had need of cash, either due to miscalculation, misfortune or misplacement – i.e. gambling losses. The most memorable visit involving Holmes's late father's gold hunter watch, for which we received 100 shillings and then placed it unwisely upon a dead certainty at Sandown Park, who promptly went down by ten lengths to the Duke of Westminster's colt, Bend Or. When we needed to recover the watch urgently the next day, guess who had to run down the road and effect an emergency recovery of said watch with the replacement security of my very own jewellery?

A sharp stab in the shin from Holmes's size ten brought me back into the room with Mr. Wilson.

'That would suit me very well' said I. 'And the pay?'

'Is four pounds per week.'

'And the work?'

'Is purely nominal.'

'What do you call purely nominal?'

'You have to be in the office, or at least the building, the whole time. If you leave, you forfeit your whole position for ever. The will is very clear upon that point. You don't comply with the conditions if you budge from the office during that time.'

'It's only four hours a day, and I should not think of leaving,' said I.

'No excuse will avail,' said Mr. Sidney Goodtime, 'neither sickness, nor business, nor anything else. There you must stay, or you will lose your billet.'

'And the work is?'

'Is to copy out the *Encyclopaedia Britannica*. There is the first volume of it in their press. You must find your own ink, pens, and blotting paper, but we will provide this table and chair. Will you be ready tomorrow?'

'Certainly,' I answered.

'Then, goodbye, Mr. Jabez Wilson, and let me congratulate you once more on the important position which you have been fortunate enough to gain.' He bowed me out of the room, and I went home with my assistant, hardly knowing what to say or do as I was so pleased at my own good fortune.'

I found Mr. Wilson extremely boring and I exhaled deeply from my subconscious. It should have acted as a cue for him to bring his story to an end but neither he nor Holmes took notice, so I jumped up and whipped out my watch accompanied by a 'My goodness, is that the time already?'

'You are so rude, sir!' said Mr. Wilson. To interrupt me on so many occasions makes me feel irrelevant. Should I continue or depart, sirs?'

'Sit down please, Watson! We can afford to miss Happy Hour for one day at least. Yes, Mr. Wilson, please continue. I sense we are only at the very beginning of your fascinating story and I must know every detail, as is my normal practice. Is that not correct, Dr. Watson?'

'Yes, Holmes…' I slumped back in my seat.

'Good. If you are sitting comfortably, Dr. Watson, I shall continue.' He cleared his throat to underline his self-importance. 'I thought over the matter all day afterwards and by the evening I was in low spirits again; for I had persuaded myself that the whole affair must be some great hoax or fraud, though what its object might be I could not imagine. It seemed altogether past belief that anyone could make such a will, or that they would pay such a sum for doing anything so simple as copying out the *Encyclopaedia Britannica*. Vincent Spaulding did what he could to cheer me up, but by bedtime I had reasoned myself out of the whole thing. However, in the morning I determined to have a look at it anyhow, so I bought a penny bottle of ink, and with a quill pen, and seven sheets of foolscap paper, I started off for Pope's Court.'

I finished off making a note of the address in my diary with a stabbing full stop, which drew the attention of both gentlemen. Holmes threw me a knowing glance and Mr. Wilson sighed even harder before continuing with his saga.

'Well, to my surprise and delight everything was as right as possible. The table and chair were set out for me, and Mr. Sidney Goodtime was there to see that I got fairly to work. He started me off upon the letter A and then he left me; but he would drop in from time to time to see that all was right with me. At two o' clock he bade me good day, complimented me upon the amount that I had written, and locked the door of the office after me.

'This went on day after day, Mr. Holmes, and on Saturday the secretary came in and plonked down four golden sovereigns for my week's work. It was the same next week, and the same the week after. Every morning I was there at ten, and every afternoon I left at two. By degrees Mr. Sidney Goodtime took to coming in only once a morning, and then after a time, he did not come in at all. Still, of course, I never dared to leave the room for an instant, for I was not sure when he might come, and the billet was such a good one, and suited me so well, that I would not risk the loss of it.

'Eight weeks passed away like this, and I had written about Abbots and Archery, and Armour, and Architecture, and Attica and hoped that with diligence that I might get on to the B's before very long. It cost me something in the foolscap, and I had pretty nearly filled a shelf with my writings. And then suddenly the whole business came to an end.'

'To an end?'

'Yes, sir. And no later than this morning. I went to work as usual at ten 'o' clock, but the door was shut and locked, with a little square of cardboard hammered onto the middle of the panel with a tack. Here it is, and you can read it for yourself.'

He held up a piece of white cardboard about the size of a sheet of notepaper. It read in this fashion: – "The Red-Headed League is dissolved. Oct 9, 1890."

Sherlock Holmes and I surveyed this curt announcement and the rueful face behind it. Then Mr. Wilson folded his arms and sat back in his chair with a conclusive stare spread across his face. There followed a pregnant silence where we looked at one another in stagnant contemplation. Eventually, Holmes raised his eyebrows towards me, which prompted me to say:

'Is that it?'

'What do you mean 'is that it?' he rasped.

Holmes's eyes sparkled as Mr. Gingernuts snatched the fly.

'Well, your story. Is *that* IT?' I repeated.

'Yes, really, IS THAT IT?' insisted Holmes.

'I really don't know what you mean!'profused an exhausted Mr. Wilson, as he reddened in the face.

'Well, IS that IT?' I repeated.

'Is THAT it, Mr. Wilson?' urged Holmes.

'I don't know what you want!' he wailed.

'IS THAT REALLY IT?! Mr. Wilson?' we chorused in unison.

'THIS IS PREPOSTEROUS!' shrieked our client (or *maybe* not our client any longer!) as he jumped up out of his chair.

'Oh, never mind' said Holmes and threw me a wicked glance to guarantee the end of our humorous routine. The problem was that Mr. Wilson's haggard features so completely over-topped every other consideration that we both burst into a roar of laughter. Unfortunately, Mr. Wilson did not possess a sense of humour. 'I cannot see that there is anything very funny!'cried our client, flushing up to the roots of his flaming head. 'If you can do nothing better than laugh at me, I can go elsewhere.'

And with that naive remark, Mr. Gingernuts strode towards the door.

'No, no,' cried Holmes, showing him back into the chair from which he had just risen. 'I really wouldn't miss your case for the world. It is most refreshingly unusual. But there is, if you will excuse me saying so, something just a little funny about it. Pray, what steps did you take when you found the card upon the door?'

'I was staggered, sir. I did not know what to do. Then I called at the offices around, but none of them seemed to know anything about it. Finally, I went to the landlord, who is an accountant living on the ground floor, and I asked him if he could tell me what had become of the Red-Headed League. He said that he had never heard of any such body. Then I asked him who Mr. Sidney Goodtime was. He answered that the name was new to him.'

"Well," I said, "it is the gentleman at No.4".

"What, the bald-headed man?"

"For goodness sakes, yes!" I said. And the fellow became quite agitated at my impetuosity.'

'I am not surprised' said Holmes. 'You hardly knew the chap, yet you were biting his head off.'

'Once I had calmed him, he told me that the red-headed man's name was William Morris. He was a solicitor and was using my room as a temporary convenience until his new premises were ready. He moved out yesterday.'

"Where could I find him?"

"Oh, at his new offices." 'He did tell me the address. Yes, 17 King Edward Street, near St Paul's.'

'I started off, Mr. Holmes, but when I got to that address it was a manufacturer of artificial knee-caps, and no-one in it had ever heard of either Mr. William Morris or Mr. Sidney Goodtime.'

'And what did you do then?' asked Holmes.

'I went to Saxe-Coburg Square, and I took the advice of my assistant. But he could not help me in any way. He could only say that if I waited, I should hear by post. But that was not quite good enough, Mr. Holmes. I did not wish to lose such a place without a struggle, so as I had heard that you were good enough to give advice to poor folk who were in need of it, I came right away to you.'

'And you did very wisely,' said Holmes. 'Your case is an exceedingly remarkable one, and I shall be happy to look into it. From what you have told me I think that it is possible that graver issues hang from it than might at first sight appear.'

'Grave enough!' said Mr. Jabez Wilson. 'Why, I have lost four pounds a week.'

'As far as you are personally concerned,' remarked Holmes, 'I do not see that you have any grievance against this extraordinary league. On the contrary, you are, as I understand, richer by some thirty pounds, to say nothing of the minute knowledge which you have gained on every subject which comes under the letter A. You have lost nothing by them.'

Mr. Wilson drew breath before responding. I took the opportunity to show him the flat of my hand thus stopping him in his tracks. I leaned forwards and tapped Holmes on the shoulder. We rose from our chairs and meandered to the side of the room, over by one of the bay windows looking out onto Baker Street. Holmes peered at me, as might an inquisitive parrot.

'What is it, Watson? What is so important? We are on the point of securing a fascinating case that puzzles me deeply.'

'Holmes, if we are taking this fellow's case, we should ask him for a proportion of his thirty pounds be rendered to us by way of an advance fee.'

'For heaven's sakes, why cause such disruption?' Holmes looked over towards Mr. Wilson who was straining every atom in his ears to learn more about our conversation. Holmes turned back to face me; he was perplexed. 'Can't you perceive that he is parsimonious beyond reason? I want this case. I need this case, for my mental capacity!' Holmes was jabbing his temple aggressively. 'This shyster, when asked for money, is about as likely to stump up an English penny as I am to take up Morris dancing. He will just walk out of that door. And I, dear Doctor, will be left with nothing to do.'

'My dear fellow, you cannot do anything anyway. We are impecunious. I have no patients in my fledgling surgery. We have spent the measly fee I was paid by *The Strand* magazine for my account of our first adventure together.'

'You spendthrift!' quipped Holmes, not taking this predicament seriously.

'Nor do we have reserves. They became exhausted after we funded the King of Bohemia affair of six months ago when we were not really paid for our services.'

'There's royalty for you!'

'Oh, I don't know, Holmes. He was most generous with his expenses. He seemed like a decent chap to me.'

This is one subject that this subject did not wish to dwell upon after the King and I had come to a candid arrangement that used his fees to settle my divorce. I would tell Holmes about it, one day.

'Our creditors are lining up at the front door; not just the butcher, the baker and candlestick maker but also the tailor and the wine merchant. We have two months of indulgence at Mother Kelly's. Soon, she will send out her bullies to settle the account.'

Holmes leaped into the stance of a bare-knuckled pugilist on-point, bobbing from foot to foot, with both fists clenched and wavering around in the space between our faces. 'They are hardly unmanageable, Watson! And even so...'

'Holmes, there is no "even so."'He continued to bob. 'You no longer receive a family stipend and my fledgling surgery is, so far, scarce on paying patients. We have barely enough cash to feed ourselves and, worst of all, we are also two months in arrears with the rent here, and you know what happens then.'

Holmes ceased to bob. 'Mrs. Hudson! Really?'

'Precisely! And you know what she is likely to do?'

Holmes hung his head in resignation, in respect of my better argument. 'I know, I know... but hush!

Don't say a word more, Watson. We are not alone.' He lifted an eyebrow towards Mr. Wilson.

I lowered my voice to a whisper. 'That is fine, Holmes, but promise me you will mention the subject of a fee, as a condition of your engagement. Please!'

Holmes sighed. He was deeply disturbed, fighting with his inner self about discussing the tacky subject of money, this being below his breeding and, most importantly, the very last distraction he desired when taking on a new case. Eventually, he started forwards towards our bemused guest and, as he passed me by, he hissed: 'Leave it to me.' He sat back down in his armchair and I followed the way back to my own.

'Mr. Holmes,' said Mr. Wilson. 'I want to find out about these rascals, who they are, and what their object was in playing this prank – if it was a prank – upon me. It was a pretty expensive joke for them, for it cost them two-and-thirty pounds.'

'Indeed, Mr. Wilson! But as the old saying goes: "a joke is never funny unless somebody is hurt or loses money," wouldn't you agree, Watson?'

'Quite so, Holmes.' I had batted an answer to my friend's question with a straight cover drive, just to get a word in edgeways, and then I stared hard at Mr. Gingernuts. 'And speaking of money, Mr. Wilson, I presume you still have that two-and-thirty pounds?'

'Watson!'

'Why yes, Doctor, I do, but what of it? Why this sudden discussion about money? Frankly, I am flabbergasted by your enquiry when my needs of Mr. Holmes's services are greater.'

'Do not remain flabbergasted, Mr. Wilson,' said Holmes. 'We shall endeavour to clear up these points for you without further ado. And first, one or two questions. This assistant of yours who first called your attention to the advertisement – how long had he been with you?'

'About a month then.'

'How did he come?'

'In answer to an advertisement.'

'Was he the only applicant?'

'No, I had a dozen.'

'Why did you pick him?'

'Because he was handy and would come cheap.'

'At half wages, in fact.'

'Yes.'

'What is he like, this Vincent Spaulding?'

'Small, stout-built, very quick in his ways, no hair on his face, though he's not short of thirty. He has a white splash of acid upon his forehead.'

Holmes sat up in his chair in considerable excitement.

'I thought as much,' said he. 'Have you ever observed that his ears are pierced for ear-rings?'

'Yes, sir, He told me that a gipsy had done it for him when he was a lad.'

'Hmmm!' hummed Holmes. 'He is still with you?'

'Oh, yes, sir. I have only just left him.'

'And has your business been attended to in your absence?'

'Nothing to complain of, sir. There's never very much to do in the morning.'

Holmes slapped the palm of his hand on the wing of his armchair. 'That will do, Mr. Wilson. I shall be happy to give you an opinion upon the subject in the course of a day or two. Today is Saturday, and I hope that by Monday we may come to a conclusion.'

With that, Holmes stood up and walked over to the fireplace where he took hold of his beaver pup pouch from its home on the mantelpiece. He opened it up and fingered some rough Turkish shag whilst pinpointing the location of his favourite churchwarden.

'Ah! I perceive this interview is over,' said Mr. Wilson. 'I shall wait to hear from you then, Mr. Holmes.' Sherlock ignored him completely. Mr. Wilson threw me a glance that told me everything I needed to know; in that he perceived my quest for money was now acute. He stood up abruptly and made a very hasty two-step towards the door. Swiftly, I calculated our fiery-headed friend's velocity and trajectory, and I intercepted him with perfect timing. He stopped in his tracks. I looked him in the eyes and said: 'Which leaves us with one final matter of business to attend to.'

'I cannot think of what that is or might be, Dr. Watson!' he lied. Then, he broke rank. He feigned a dive to the left of me but then jinxed and darted forwards to the right. Memories came flooding back of my days in the ring, but not quickly enough because he had passed me in a trice and pounced onto the doorknob like a jungle cat. I turned as quickly as I could but that old jezail bullet wound shrieked a terrible, jabbing pain up into my groin. It was a thunderbolt into the cobblers! As he wrenched the door open, I assessed his advantage and gave up the chase. The best I could manage was a lacklustre 'Hoy!' as he disappeared from view and scuttled down the staircase. As I watched on, with Holmes behind me, the striking of a match broke the silence and, as a waft of heavy pipe smoke permeated the atmosphere, I suffered the inevitable.

'Ha! What did I tell you, dear Doctor?!' He laughed some more. I turned around to see him leaned casually against the mantelpiece pup-pup-pupping on his pipe to encourage full ignition. 'What do you make of it all?'

'I make nothing of it, 'I answered, frankly. 'It is a most mysterious business.'

'As a rule,' said Holmes, 'the most bizarre the thing is the less mysterious it proves to be. It is your commonplace, featureless crimes which are really puzzling, just as a commonplace face is the most difficult to identify. But I must be prompt over this matter.'

'What are you going to do then?' I asked.

'To smoke,' he answered. 'It is quite a three-pipe problem, and I beg that you won't speak to me for fifty minutes.' He curled himself up in his chair, with his thin knees drawn up to his hawk-like nose, and there he sat with his eyes closed and his walnut churchwarden thrusting out like the bill of some strange bird. I had come to the conclusion that he had dropped to asleep, and indeed was nodding off myself, when he suddenly sprang out of his chair with the gesture of a man who had made up his mind, and put his pipe down upon the mantelpiece.

'Sarasate plays at the St. James's Hall this afternoon,' he remarked. 'What do you think, Watson? Could your patients spare you for a few hours?'

'Patients? What did I say just now, Holmes? My practice is completely and utterly devoid of any patients. I have nothing to do today.'

'Good! Then put on your hat and come. I am going through the City first, and we can have some lunch on the way. I observe that there is a good deal of German music on the programme, which is rather more to my taste than Italian or French. It is introspective, and I wish to be introspect. Come along!'

And all of this, dear reader, would have to be paid out of the two shillings and fourpence I had accumulated over the past few days; indeed, I knew that it was inadequate for a trip around London by hansom cab, a five-courser in a swish dining room and the privilege of access to one of the world's virtuoso violinists for the afternoon, but before I could register a protest Holmes had donned his frock coat and topper, and plucked his favourite swordstick from the Pocahontas rack. I stared at him for a moment, his eyes twinkling, his demeanour tense and oozing vitality. Here was a magnificent example of *homo sapiens* portrayed in sheer exuberance, as excited as a virgin schoolboy on the doorstep of a fine Parisian knocking-shop with five pounds in his pocket. I simply couldn't bring myself to pop his balloon with the needle of impecunity. He marched towards the door with a spring in his step.

'Coming Holmes!' I cried. I grabbed my hat and followed him out of the apartment.

* * *

We travelled by Underground as far as Aldersgate; and a short walk took us to Saxe-Coburg Square, the scene of the singular story which we had listened to in the morning. It was a pokey, shabby-genteel place, where four lines of dingy two-storied brick houses looked out into a small railed-in enclosure, here a lawn of weedy grass and a few clumps of faded laurel bushes made a hard fight against a smoke-laden and uncongenial atmosphere. Three gilt balls and a brown board with 'JABEZ WILSON' in white letters, upon a corner house, announced the place where our ginger-nutted client carried on his business. Sherlock Holmes stopped in front of it with his head on one side and looked it all over, with his eyes shining brightly between puckered lids. I observed and I marvelled at the man whose constitution suffered no end of substance abuse during days of cocooned inactivity, but when the bell tolled, and his hour of need cometh, the true detective emerged as a new butterfly from its crisp chrysalis, flying high on a warm summer's breeze.

Holmes walked slowly up the street and then down again to the corner, still looking keenly at the houses. Finally, he returned to the pawnbroker's, and, having thumped vigorously upon the pavement with his stick two or three times he went up to the door and knocked. It was instantly opened by a bright-looking, clean-shaven young fellow, who asked him to step in.

'Thank you,' said Holmes, 'I only wished to ask you how you would go from here to The Strand.'

'Third right, fourth left,' answered the assistant promptly, closing the door.

'Smart fellow, that,' observed Holmes as we walked away.

'Quite frankly, Holmes, I am surprised he didn't tell you where to go.'

'Well, in fact, he did.'

'That's not what I mean! Wasting his time answering the door for simple directions that one could

Was Sherlock Holmes imitating the mating call of the green woodpecker?

have gleaned easily from a street urchin? If I was him, having been disturbed so unnecessarily, I would have told you to go all right – go forth and multiply! That is what I mean!'

'Luckily, Watson, the fellow is too smart to let his emotions over-rule his integrity. He is, in my judgment, the fourth smartest man in London, and for daring I am not sure that he has not a claim to be third. I have known something of him before.'

'Evidently,' said I, 'Mr. Wilson's assistant counts for a good deal in this mystery of the Red-headed League. I am sure that you enquired your way merely in order that you might see him.'

'Not him.'

'Really? What, then?'

'The knees of his trousers.'

'And, what did you see?'

'What I expected to see.'

The great detective was in a mood of infuriating obtuseness. I made the mistake of forcing out an unrehearsed rebuke. 'So, it's a game, is it?' He could sense the frustration in the timbre of my voice and took advantage. He waved his silver-topped ebony cane at me airily and smiled his broadest grin.

'The game's afoot, Watson!'

'That is as may be, Holmes, but at least let me know why you beat the pavement?'

'My dear Doctor, this is a time for observation, not for talk. We are spies in an enemy's country. We know something of Saxe-Coburg Square. Let us now explore the paths which lie behind it.' And he marched ahead.

The road in which we found ourselves as we turned around the corner from the retired Saxe-Coburg Square presented as a great a contrast to it as the front of a picture does to the back. It was one of the main arteries which convey the traffic of the City to the north and west. The roadway was blocked with the immense stream of commerce flowing in a double tide inward and outwards, while the footpaths were black with the hurrying swarm of pedestrians. It was difficult to realize as we looked at the line of fine shops and stately business premises that they really abutted on the other side upon the faded and stagnant square which we had just quitted.

'Let me see'said Holmes, standing at the corner, and glancing along the line, 'I should like just to remember the order of the houses here. It is a hobby of mine to have an exact knowledge of London. There is Mortimer's, the tobacconist, the little newspaper shop, the Coburg branch of the City and Suburban Bank, the Vegetarian Restaurant, and McFarlane's carriage building depot. That carries us right onto the other block.'

'The veggie restaurant is the obvious nigger in the woodpile, Holmes. I ask you: who in their right mind would dedicate their life to just eating vegetables? It is preposterous! I presume you perceive, like me, for it to be a diversion for some unknown criminal organisation. Maybe you could enlighten me about the relevance of these business premises?'

Holmes chuckled to himself smugly. 'Not now, Watson! We have done our work, so it's time we had some play.'

'I can tell you right now, Holmes, we will not be playing very hard with a couple of shillings to our names!'

'If our resources are limited, we shall find a simple sandwich and a bottle of house claret. Then, we shall be ready to go off to violin land, where all is sweetness, and delicacy, and harmony, and there are no red-headed clients to vex us with their conundrums.'

I took a moment to contemplate the rest of this day's agenda, especially as I was not an enthusiastic musician or lover of music. What with my friend's blind enthusiasm blocking my layman enquiries and the thought of being forced to suffer the scrapings of over tightened catgut for the whole afternoon I had a sudden urge to drink claret of the bin end variety in copious quantities. I discarded my reservation about our impecunious state and hailed a cab.

'To the George and Vulture!'

As we mounted the hansom, Holmes tipped his topper to me. 'That is more like it, Doctor! Here's to a fine table and a convivial ambience.' We sat back in the cab and clattered off towards Cornhill.

It was a beautiful autumnal day in the City, and I marvelled at the array of gentlemen going about their business dressed in black morning coat, some wearing bowlers but most with fine, shiny top hats. Here, in the very hub of the industrial world, one could see the army of earnest civilians that drove the cut and thrust of big business; merchant bankers, commodity traders, insurance-wallahs taking their slice of the pie. Apparently, my Great Uncle Eric worked here somewhere; according to my late mother, he was a banker of some description, heaven knows where, but I can only recall one or two images of him in the year that he was invited one Christmas Day to join us in the family celebrations. I was a very young boy at that time, probably four years old. I remember him as a tall, thin man with a beaky nose, very well dressed and, come to think of it, dear reader, he was a gingernut too! He had a rather nervous disposition. He would lunge in very close to those he wished to speak to, and then start each sentence with a little stutter, his frame shaking ever so slightly, arms bobbing up and down, as if he was being operated from above by a novice marionettist, with one hand always clasping a burning cigarette. Before luncheon, he took great pleasure in handing out festive cards to me and my siblings. When it was my turn, he bent down and thrust his face to within an inch of mine and, amidst curling plumes of cigarette smoke, placed a large, white envelope into my hand and said:

"Hee...he-he-he...HEE-YAR's wishing yoo a veery hairrrpy krrristmass Johnnn!"

Did I forget to mention he was from Dundee?

"D..d...DOONT frrrritter-it-a'way ay a' once, yer wee rascal! S...s...save a bob o'two fer wine, women and song!"

He chuckled himself puce at his own joke and ruffled my hair, as he did with all of us children. I can still remember my brothers and sisters and I tearing open our envelopes in front of the tree, watched upon intently by Uncle Eric and my parents. Inside, there was a card bearing the wintry scene of The Bank of England, all covered in snow with Santa Claus himself flying high on his sleigh above the City skyline. But the big surprise was yet to come – when we opened our cards a brand new ten-shilling note jumped out and fluttered to the floor! We all gasped and capered at the sight of such a large sum of money landing in front of us. Uncle Eric took enormous pleasure from fielding our unbridled pipings of gratitude. Yes, now I come to think about it, I reckon Uncle Eric was a very successful banker and led a pretty comfortable lifestyle, a remarkable figurehead in the Watson family. I decided to relay these happy memories to Holmes, to break the silence in the coach and initiate a casual conversation. I looked over at him; he had his eyes closed and his head tilted back against the studded leather seat.

'I say, Holmes, did I ever tell you about my Great Uncle...'

'Eric? Beaky nose? Ginger? Quivers like a catholic bride on her wedding night? Is a banker here in the City? Gave you ten-shillings one Christmas? Yes, you did. Twice. Now, I am in deep pontification, Watson. Please keep quiet.'

I suppose it was just as well. He would only have picked holes in my story and asked questions that I couldn't answer, and then he would show off by telling me what Uncle Eric had for breakfast today! Besides, a few minutes later, we arrived at our destination. Holmes jumped out onto Lombard Street and headed down an alley towards the George & Vulture. I paid the cab man. After a brief debate with him about the etiquette of tipping, I followed the great detective through a deeply recessed doorway into the ancient building. The wooden atrium was the smallest of spaces, what with a staircase, two doorways and a cloakroom there wasn't enough room to fit a lone, fat man, let alone myself, Holmes, an obese serving wench, and the Maître d', Senor Julio Inglesias, a swarthy individual of high-octane Latin descent. He shouted a very warm welcome and ushered us through to the Dining Room.

We squeezed through the doorway and once we had gathered ourselves together, Holmes collared Inglesias before he could start lathering us up with his exuberant bonhomie.

'My dear Senor Julio, I see that you have just returned from Oporto where you celebrated your father's 80th birthday for seven days and seven nights.'

Inglesias threw up his arms in ecstasy and cried out, so loudly that the whole restaurant stopped eating. 'MEESTER HOLMES! This is AAA-BSO-LOOO-TLEY, per-fect-ly TRUE! You SEE into my very SOUL! It is COMPLEET meestery to me HOW do you do thees? How do you know thees to be SO?!'

The entire restaurant's clientele was in silence, hanging in anticipation of my friend's explanation. Holmes could see that Inglesias had captured an audience and he must now put on a performance of superior quality. Holmes came to life, all of a sudden, with energy radiating from his face, his feet planted on the spot and his tall frame wavering like a merry flower in hot sunshine.

'It is elementary, my dear Maître d'! I spy three cases of Quinta Da Noval port wine over there, propped up against the wall. They were not here the last time I visited. They are estancia bottled. As all port is shipped to London in clay pipes and then bottled here for distribution, these must have accompanied you on a recent return from Oporto. They were also a birthday present to your father, for I see a card fixed to the side of one box with the inscription:

"Feliz Aniversario, Ronaldo! O seu, em seu 80, sua velha boceta!"

There was a sudden shriek of laughter and a hard slap of the table from a black-haired gentleman at table in the far corner. Inglesias shifted nervously from one foot to the other – he knew what the inscription meant – but I didn't because I am ignorant of the Portuguese lingo. The same went the other diners because they just murmured and pointed at the dark gentleman. I suspected it was a ribald note of extreme vulgarity. Inglesias gestured the diners to settle down again and Holmes picked up from where he had left off.

'Then, I see that you have a gold ring on your fifth finger that features the Inglesias coat of arms. This ring, Senor Julio, is a recent addition to your array of daytime jewellery and must, therefore, be a family heirloom passed to you as his eldest son, which can only have been on his deathbed. As most Portuguese anniversary celebrations continue for about one week, I perceive he celebrated his milestone to his heart's content in the bosom of his family, but then the extreme overindulgence overcame his frail constitution. You, Senor Julio, are not melancholy about his passing because you were with him when his time came, and you saw him drift off in bliss.'

Inglesias leapt in the air and clapped his hands. 'BEM FEITO, Mr. Holmes!' he cried, and the clientele broke into sudden, but brief, applause, the majority undoubtedly wanting to end this bumptious sideshow and eat their luncheons. The great detective took a bow that was modestly graceful. However, there was no stopping Inglesias, who danced capriciously from one foot to the other whilst clapping his hands above his head and shouting 'BEM FEITO! BEM FEITO!' over and over again. He rousted the restaurant's serving wenches to join in the celebration and soon we could hear 'ooh, ain't he the clever one!' and 'it's that 'andsome detective come again!' and 'get him!'

Then, from the other side of the room, a well-tonsured man stood up. He glared at us and barked: 'Will you please keep the noise down? We wish to hold an *intellectual* conversation over here and we cannot hear ourselves speak!'

Holmes cracked a smile and rebuked the man jovially. 'Who the Dickens do you think you are? If you cannot hear your friend's voice with adequate clarity, maybe you should find yourself an ear trumpet?'

To my surprise, the man burst out laughing and then sat down in his seat. His friend also laughed and waved two fingers at us in a gesture of friendly defiance. As we were ushered to a prominent table on the left-hand side of the room, the diners resumed their meals and the restaurant returned to a burble of hushed conversations and occasional exclamations. We were handed menus by one of the wenches. Holmes seized his copy and studied it immediately.

'Holmes, what do you make of Mr. Gingernuts' predicament?' I enquired.

He ran his eye over the dishes on offer and replied with impatience. 'There is a strong connection between the business of Mr. Jabez Wilson and Saxe-Coburg Square, but not with Mr. Wilson playing the protagonist. He is merely a pawn in a grand game of chess that is going on right under our noses.'

'Really? I didn't know that.'

'No, you didn't, Watson. The jigsaw puzzle is still being constructed in my head. Who the main players are I cannot be sure of yet? However, you can be certain that they are not far away.'

I cast my eye around the gentlemen diners. 'Maybe they are in this very room, my friend? Although, I cannot see any likely candidates. No, maybe those two characters over there.' I nodded towards the well-tonsured man and his dining companion. 'They look shifty.'

Holmes sighed with despair. It seems that I was on the wrong tack. 'Dear me, Watson, they are writers, and notorious ones at that. That is their natural appearance. The impertinent one is Mr. Wilde and the sign-language expert is Mr. Hardy.'

'I have never even heard of them, Holmes, but if you say so it will be thus. Reverting to the conversation about this mystery of ours, have you given any thought to the reconnaissance of the neighbourhood behind the Square?'

'Yes, indeed, I have, Watson. That is one of the most important aspects of our work today which requires an injection of energy, and it is why I am heading towards the double Barnsley Chop with a plate of oysters to slip down prior and whet my appetite. Waiter!'

Once we had ordered our food, and we had just about money left from the two shillings and fourpence – minus hansom fare, no tip – for a Medoc of classed growth quality, I resumed my probing of the great detective's mind.

'If you ask me, the vegetarian restaurant is the sinister connection to Mr. Wilson's business.'

'I would not dream of asking you, dear Doctor! Nor would I ever contemplate asking for your deductions when you have made such an absurd connection. Tell me, what exactly is this link that you have made between the restaurant and Mr. Gingernuts?'

'I tell you Holmes, it is not so much the connection; it is the *disconnection* of such an establishment being even in existence. It is quite fantastical to imagine that there is a sustainable business in offering just vegetables to paying customers. I state, quite categorically, as a Doctor of Medicine in general practice both here in London, and in the Hindu Kush, that good old *homo sapiens*, we human beings, cannot survive on vegetables alone. We must eat meat to garner iodine, calcium and vitamins.'

'A, D and B12, I believe?'

His scope, as usual, was way beyond the normal range of most people. I nodded acknowledgement – that is all he was going to get – before I continued my specialist lecture. 'Otherwise, the brain, robbed of its essential elements, becomes confused,' I said. 'In a nutshell, the patient goes off their rocker. Also, the effectiveness of the body's immune system is reduced severely. The quality of the skin deteriorates and becomes pallid. Worst of all, the person becomes delusional and fools themselves into thinking they are healthy, sometimes better off than their omnivore bedfellows, and tries to convert his nearest and dearest to also being vegetarians. Therefore, the restaurant located behind Saxe-Coburg Square IS the number one suspect in this mystery. I stake my reputation upon it!'

Holmes stared at me; his blue-grey-green eyes boring deeply into mine. Suddenly, he snatched the bottle from the table, which was devoid of claret, and held it high above our heads. 'Inglesias! Mais deste plonk Portuguese!' The black-haired fellow from earlier looked up and shouted: 'Ouca! Ouca! Senhor!' And Holmes lobbed the bottle across the room to the

Maître d', who caught it like a first-rate cricketer. Being Portuguese, poor fellow, that was someone he could never be.

* * *

We slipped into St. James's Hall through the lavatory window, thus avoiding the box office. My friend was an enthusiastic musician, being himself not only a very capable performer, but a composer of no ordinary merit. All the afternoon he sat in the stalls wrapped in the most perfect happiness, gently waving his long thin fingers in time to the music, while his gently smiling face and his languid, dreamy eyes were as unlike those of Holmes the sleuth-hound, Holmes the relentless, keen-witted, ready handed, criminal agent, as it was possible to conceive. In his singular character the dual nature alternately asserted itself, and his extreme exactness and astuteness represented, as I have often thought, the reaction against the poetic and contemplative mood which occasionally predominated in him. The swing of his nature took him from extreme languor to devouring energy; and, as I knew well, he was never so truly formidable as when, for days on end, he had been lounging in his armchair amid his improvisations and his black-letter editions. Then it was that the lust of the chase would suddenly come upon him, and that his brilliant reasoning power would rise to the level of intuition, until those who were unacquainted with his methods would look askance at him as on a man whose knowledge was not that of other mortals. When I saw him that afternoon, so enwrapped in the music at St. James's Hall I felt that an evil time might be coming upon those whom he had set himself to hunt down.

'Even though you have had a good sleep, you want to go home, no doubt, Doctor?' he remarked, as we emerged.

'Yes, it would be as well.'

'And I have some business to do which will take some hours. This business at Coburg Square is serious.'

'Why serious?'

'Watson, all crime is a serious business! But, regardless of the maxim, this red-headed business is more than the common man might think it is.'

'That's me, Holmes, the common man!' You see, dear reader, there was method in my humility. I liked to act out my role in the duo in a benign way in order to elicit as much information from the great man as possible, such knowledge being all the better for these written accounts of our adventures together. I knew that Holmes liked to assert his superior intellect over me at every opportunity. My friend enjoyed to brag – he must have been blessed with Anglo Saxon genes – and this was to my advantage because it would make my chronicles more valuable.

'In other words,' he continued, 'there is a considerable crime in contemplation. I have every reason to believe that we shall be in time to stop it. But today being Saturday rather complicates matters. I shall want your help tonight.'

'At what time?'

'Ten will be early enough.'

'I will return to my surgery now to continue tutoring my new practice secretary. I have no plans for this evening. I shall be at Baker Street well before ten.'

‘Very well. And, I say, Doctor, there may be some little danger, so kindly put your army revolver in your pocket.’ He waved his hand, turned on his heel, and disappeared in an instant among the crowd.

What army revolver?

* * *

I trust that I am not denser than my neighbours, but I was always oppressed with a sense of my own stupidity in my dealings with Sherlock Holmes. Here I had heard what he had heard, I had seen what he had seen, and yet from his words it was evident that he saw clearly not only what had happened, but what was about to happen, while to me the whole business was still confused and grotesque. Being completely skinned of all of my cash, I was obliged to walk back towards my medical practice in Kensington, an ambulation that took me over an hour, which gave me ample time to think over it all, from the extraordinary story of the red-headed copier of the *Encyclopaedia* down to the visit to Saxe-Coburg Square, and the ominous words with which he had parted from me. What was this nocturnal expedition, and why should I go armed? Where were we going, and what were we to do? I had the hint from Holmes that this smooth faced pawnbroker’s assistant was a formidable man – a man who might play a deep game. I tried to puzzle it out, but gave up in despair, and set the matter aside until night should bring an explanation. The matter in hand was the search and acquisition of an army revolver within the next three hours. Where, on Earth, or in London, was I to find one in such a short period of time?

Once back in my medical rooms, I went through the appointment register with my new practice secretary, my sister's boy, a teenage lad named Will. The following day looked very promising with four new clients in the book, all due to my nephew's endeavour. Praise where praise is due! I needed to encourage the lad. I poured a glass of madeira and handed it to the youngster, along with a stirring message.

'Well done William! Things are looking up. Tell me, just how did you find these new consultations? Did you carry out my instructions to market my unique bedside manner to these new patrons, as I advised you?'

He looked a little quizzical, for a second, and then was quite determined in his reply. 'Oh yes,' he said, 'that is precisely what I did. And if these new patrons turn out to be regular consultations, which I think they will, I am confident of delivering many more.'

I clinked glasses with the young shaver whilst reflecting upon the commission I had inspired the boy with this morning as being a sight too rich. 'Indeed? Here's to you, Will. Tell me, how did you find these people in the first place? What special source have you discovered?'

'It is from a very special place, Uncle. Very nearby.'

'Excellent, my boy! And would you be able to reveal the identity of your Aladdin's Cave?'

'Yes, but all in good time, Uncle.'

He needed loosening up. I went to pour him a refill but, all of a sudden, he looked flustered and placed his hand across the opening.

'If you will excuse me, Uncle John, I must make tracks homewards, as a matter of urgency. My dear

William needed to earn money to buy himself some long trousers

mother, your dearest sister, is stricken with influenza and I am the only one of her dutiful children to nurse her.'

He spoke the truth. His siblings had all died. How could I say no? He swigged the remains of his drink and bid me good evening as he gathered up his overcoat and hat. I walked him to the door and patted him upon his shoulders whilst reminding him of his excellent work that day. Then, I had a sudden reminder of my immediate predicament and called a halt to his exit.

'I say, you are a young fellow, you will be more in touch with the *underground* in the *grass roots* division of this neighbourhood. You wouldn't happen to know where I could acquire a revolver, would you?'

William stopped in his tracks and pondered a moment. 'Why yes, sir. The gunmaker, Boss & Sons, is just down the road. There is none finer in the neighbourhood, but I would hasten your purchase because it is already a quarter past five and the shop closes in fifteen minutes. I shall return tomorrow in good time greet the first of our new patients. Good evening to you, Uncle.'

William slipped out of the door. Dammit! I had been hoping that he might reveal a source that may be described amongst the lower orders as *under-the-counter* and he hadn't sensed my enquiry in the way I would have liked. Ah, the innocence of youth! I had two pence ha'penny to my name, way below the hundred or so guineas required to purchase a new revolver from the likes of Boss & Sons. I would have to think of something else. Luckily, I did.

* * *

It was a quarter past nine when I started from Kensington. I had scrubbed my nails and fingers clean of any black paint residue. I was not in the habit of lying to anybody, but my conscience would permit a small deception. If I was to hide the secret of this unusual revolver from the great Sherlock Holmes successfully, I could not be seen to have even one speck of paint on my hands.

I made my way across the Park, and through the eyesore known as Oxford Street – I recently referred to it to Holmes as "the bum crack of London" within earshot of Mrs. Hudson and received a clip around the ear for my language – and finally onto Baker Street. Two hansoms were standing at the door, and, as I entered the passage, I looked out for Mrs. Hudson. She would make life extremely difficult until she was paid the rent arrears up to date but, luckily, it seemed she was out elsewhere. I heard the sound of voices from above. On entering the room, I found Holmes in animated conversation with two men, one of whom I recognised as Peter Jones. No, dear reader, not the shopkeeper out near Knightsbridge, but the police agent. The other was a long, thin, sad faced man, with a very shiny hat and a frock coat of admirably fine quality.

'Ha! Our party is complete,' said Holmes, buttoning up his pea jacket, and taking his heavy hunting crop from the rack. 'Watson, I think you know Mr. Jones, of Scotland Yard? Let me introduce you to Mr. Merryweather, who is to be our companion in tonight's adventure.'

I was stunned. Wasn't I supposed to be his companion in this adventure? For that matter, in *any* adventure? It was Holmes and Watson, not Holmes and Mister whoever-you-think-you-are-mister-Merryweather. The policeman, Mr. Jones, deciphered my features like he was reading the front page of The Times.

'There, there, Doctor, do not fret. This is only a temporary arrangement. We're hunting in couples again, you see,' said Jones in his consequential way. 'Our friend here is a wonderful man for starting a chase. All he wants is an old dog to help him to do the running down.'

'I hope a wild goose may not prove to be the end of our chase,' observed Mr. Merryweather gloomily.

I told him my thoughts on the subject without hesitation. 'Please excuse my look of surprise. I was not aware of an additional companion for this evening's operation. However, I do not understand why we require the assistance a of a dog and a goose. Mr. Holmes and I do not employ such fanciful accessories in our operations. It is confusing, to say the least.'

'Well, sir, I am ever so slightly confused,' said Mr. Merryweather. 'Which dog and goose do you refer to, Doctor? I cannot see any. Mr. Jones?'

'What about a dog and goose?' said Jones. This conversation was one of those crossed over misunderstandings that become nonsensical and should have been taking place in an asylum. It was Merryweather who brought it to an end, and he showed his true colours at the same time. He moved in closer to the police agent and lowered his voice. 'I know nothing about these animals, but I have my doubts about this particular arrangement. As to why we have these civilians with us, working alongside professional police detectives, is a complete mystery to me. Why is it, Mr. Jones? What do they add to this evening's mission?'

Merryweather made scant effort to muffle his voice, which turned him into a buffoon in my eyes because we could hear every word he said. I flicked my eyes over to Holmes. His features had darkened considerably; any attempt to cast dispersion upon his ability was always met with anger and, then, violence. I noticed a reddening of his cheeks, a tightening of his lips and a clenching of his hands, a sure sign that he was boiling up into a rage. I stepped in smartly and held up my hands.

'Now, now, now, Mr. Merryweather!' I said. 'I think that you have underestimated our qualifications.'

'Indeed so, Doctor Watson!' interjected the police agent loftily. Jones knew that Holmes had a tendency to be pugnacious when riled, and he looked worried. 'Mr. Merryweather, you may place considerable confidence in Mr. Holmes. He has his own little methods, which are, if you don't mind my saying so, just a little too theatrical and fantastic, but he has the makings of a detective in him. It is not too much to say that once or twice, as in that business of the Sholto murder and the Agra treasure, he has been more nearly correct than the official force.'

'Oh, if you say so, Mr. Jones, it is all right!' said the stranger, with deference.

'And so, it should be!' barked Holmes. 'Sholto was all my own work. The treasure was restored to its rightful owner due to my sole intervention. And today, if it wasn't for my reputation as the world's greatest private detective...'

'*Only* private detective!' I corrected.

'Thank you, Watson,' he stutter-seethed, and drew himself up, 'IF it wasn't for my reputation as the world's *only great* private detective and my unique conclusions drawn from the interview of Mr. Jabez Wilson, come the dawn of tomorrow morning, you would have egg all over your face. And as for the police involvement, think yourself lucky enough that I dropped in on Mr. Jones and invited him along this evening. Otherwise you would not even be here, Mr. Merryweather. You would be playing bridge.'

Merryweather jumped up out of his chair, his face wrought in wonder. 'But just HOW could you know that I was playing bridge tonight?!'

'Ha, Mr. Banker! I exclaimed. Put that in your pipe and smoke it!' How could I resist?

Holmes changed his mood as rapidly as Merryweather changed his. Now, instead of anger, the broadest of grins spread across his handsome features. Mr. Merryweather dropped his arms to his sides, desolated and defeated by the great detective's insight.

'I cannot imagine how a complete stranger has such an accurate awareness of my private life. I am shocked to the core, Mr. Holmes! I can see now why Jones admires your talents. Also, I can see that I have offended you both.'

'Not as much as Jones here!' quipped Holmes.

'Still, I have made my opinions obvious, and I apologise. I confess that I am a touch unsettled because I shall miss my rubber. It is the first Friday night for seven-and-twenty years that I have not had my rubber.'

I must have been wearing an empty expression because Sherlock Holmes stared at me. 'Bridge, Watson, bridge! The very epitome of a card game.' Then, he turned his attention back to Mr. Merryweather. 'I think you will find that you will play for a higher stake tonight than you have ever done yet, and that the play will be more exciting. For you, Mr. Merryweather, the stake will be some thirty thousand pounds; and for you, Jones, it will be the man upon whom you have wished to lay your hands for many years and, thus, the admonishments from your superior officers will cease from this night on.'

'Indeed, Mr. Holmes,' replied Jones. 'John Clay, the murderer, thief, smasher, and forger. He's a young man, Mr. Merryweather, but he is at the head of his profession, and I would rather have my bracelets on him than on any criminal in London. He's a remarkable man, is young John Clay. His grandfather was a Royal Duke, and he himself has been to Eton and Oxford. His brain is as cunning as his fingers, and though we meet signs of him at every turn, we never know where to find the man himself. He'll crack a crib in Scotland one week and be raising money to build an orphanage in Cornwall the next. I've been on his track for years and have never set eyes on him yet.'

'I hope that I have the pleasure of introducing you tonight. I've had one or two little turns also with Mr. John Clay, and I agree with you that he is at the head of his profession. It is past ten, however, and quite time we started. If you two will take the first hansom, Watson, I will follow in the second.'

Sherlock Holmes was not very communicative during the long drive and lay back in the cab humming the tunes which he had heard in the afternoon. We rattled through an endless labyrinth of gas lit streets until we emerged into Farringdon Street.

'We are close there now,' my friend remarked. He sat up and leaned over close to me. 'This fellow Merryweather is a bank director and personally interested in the matter. I thought it as well to have Jones with us also. He is not a bad fellow, though an absolute imbecile in his profession. He has one positive virtue. He is as brave as a bulldog, and as tenacious as a lobster, if he gets his claws upon anyone.'

'Holmes, please would you help me clear my mind? Could you let me know why there are so many animals in this adventure and I have yet to see even one of them?'

He stared at me, for what seemed like a very long period of time. It was as if he wanted to tell me something very important, but he couldn't open his mouth to say the words. Then, the hansom driver could be heard entreating his horse to a halt and Holmes broke the spell by averting his gaze with a look outside the cab. 'Ah! Here we are, and they are waiting for us.'

We had reached the same crowded thoroughfare in which we had found ourselves in the morning. Our cabs were dismissed, and, following the guidance of Mr. Merryweather, we passed down a narrow passage, and through a side door, which he opened for us. Within there was a small corridor, which ended in a very massive iron gate. This also was opened, and led down a flight of winding stone steps, which terminated at another formidable gate. Mr. Merryweather stopped to light a lantern, and then conducted us down a dark, earth-smelling passage, and so, after opening a third door, into a huge vault or cellar, which was piled all around with crates and massive boxes.

'You are not very vulnerable from above,' Holmes remarked, as he held up the lantern and gazed about him.

'Nor from below,' said Mr. Merryweather, striking his stick upon the flags which lined the floor. 'Why, dear me, it sounds quite hollow!' he remarked, looking up in surprise.

'I really must ask you to be a little quieter,' said Holmes severely. 'You have already imperilled the whole success of our expedition. Might I beg that you would have the goodness to sit down upon one of those boxes, and not to interfere?'

The solemn Mr. Merryweather perched himself upon a crate, with a very injured expression upon his face. He flicked his eyes towards me. I sniffed and turned my back upon him. Holmes fell upon his knees upon the floor, and, with the lantern and a magnifying lens, began to examine minutely the cracks between the stones. A few seconds sufficed to satisfy him, for he sprang to his feet again, and put his glass in his pocket.

'We have at least an hour before us,' he remarked, 'for they can hardly take any steps until the good pawnbroker is safely in bed. Then they will not lose a minute, for the sooner they do their work the longer time they will have for their escape. We are at present, Doctor – as no doubt you have divined – in the cellar of the City branch of one of our principal London banks. Mr. Merryweather is the chairman of directors, and he will explain to you that there are reasons why the more daring criminals of London should take a considerable interest in this cellar at present.'

'It is our French gold,' whispered the director. 'We have had several warnings that an attempt might be made upon it.'

'Your French gold?'

'Yes, we had occasion some months ago to strengthen our resources, and borrowed, for that purpose, thirty thousand napoleons from the Bank of France. It has become known that we have never had occasion to unpack the money, and that it is still lying in our cellar. The crate upon which I sit contains two thousand napoleons packed between layers of lead foil. Our reserve of bullion is much larger at present than is usually kept in a single branch office, and the directors have had misgivings upon the subject.'

'Which were very well justified,' observed Holmes. 'And now it is time that we arranged our little plans. I expect that within an hour matters will come to a head. In the meantime, Mr. Merryweather, we must put the screen over that dark lantern.'

'And sit in the dark?'

'I am afraid so. I had brought a pack of cards in my pocket, and I thought that, as we were a *partie carrée*, you might have your rubber after all. But I see that the enemy's preparations have gone so far that we cannot risk the presence of a light. And, first of all, we must choose our positions. These are daring men, and, though we shall take them at a disadvantage they may do us some harm, unless we are careful. I shall stand behind this crate, and you conceal yourself behind those. Then, when I flash a light upon them, close in swiftly. If they fire, Watson, have no compunction about shooting them down. You have remembered to bring that revolver of yours?'

'It is more of a pistol, Holmes,' I answered.

'That is no difference. Either a pistol or revolver will do, perchance a pistol is more practical in these confines. May we see it?'

'It will be my pleasure.'

'Then why are you moving away from us, Doctor?'

I had taken one or two steps back into the shadows where clear sight would be more difficult. I drew the painted water pistol from my inside coat pocket. I made a big show of pretending to cock the mechanism. 'There's one in the chamber now!' I shouted. I adopted the stance of a crime fighter and then I whipped my body around one hundred and eighty degrees and aimed at my assembled group of colleagues.

'Bang! Bang! You are dead!'

'Precisely, Watson!' cried Holmes. 'You must shoot to kill. These villains are just as ruthless.' But I noticed Merryweather catch Jones's eye with an anxious face. Whilst still in the subdued light I replaced the trusty toy into my pocket as Holmes declared: 'Now, your positions please, gentlemen.'

Jones withdrew to one side of the room and hid behind a pillar, Holmes to the opposite side. That left me and Mr. Merryweather to locate ourselves behind a pile of the cases containing the napoleons. Holmes shot the slide across the front of his lantern and left us in pitch darkness – such an absolute darkness as I have never before experienced. The smell of hot metal remained to assure us that the light was still there, ready to flash out at a moment's notice.

Beside me, Mr. Merryweather touched my shoulder and lent into my ear and hissed: 'I cannot believe what I am seeing. A doctor, of medicine no less, who is hell bent with intent to shoot dead a perfectly healthy human being without charge or trial!'

I scarcely believed what I had just heard. What an oaf this bank director was turning out to be. To me, with my nerves worked up to a pitch of expectancy, there was something depressing and subduing in the sudden gloom, and in the cold, dark air of the vault but to have this fool making crass remarks to me about my loyalty to Hippocrates was going one step too far. However, the rise in my temperature stalled for a moment whilst the great detective double-checked with the policeman that all aspects were secure.

'I say, Jones. They have but one retreat,' whispered Holmes. 'That is back through the house into Saxe-Coburg Square. I hope that you have done what I asked you?'

'I have an inspector and two officers waiting at the front door.'

'Good. Then we have stopped all the holes. And now we must be silent and wait.'

What a time it seemed! From comparing notes afterwards, it was but an hour and a quarter, yet it appeared to me that the night must have almost gone, and the dawn be breaking above us. It gave me time to think about how I may exact my revenge against Merryweather for his pious criticisms. Inspiration arrived later than expected, only when I cast my mind back to my schooldays. I remembered something unique to my physiology that I hadn't played out for ages and was very much a talking-point amongst my fellow students all those years ago. There are some freaks of nature amongst us: some people can bend a finger onto the back of the hand; others can extend their tongue to touch their forehead. My genetic talent started by swallowing mouthfuls of air and holding my breath. I had to concentrate very intensely on my constitution, and then move my body into the correct position, but my limbs were weary and stiff. I feared to change that position, but I must, just a fraction, to execute the action. My nerves were worked up to the highest pitch of tension, and my hearing was so acute that I could not only hear the gentle breathing of my companions, but I could distinguish the deeper, heavier in-breath of the bulky Jones from one side of the room and the thin, sighing note of the bank director beside me. All of a sudden, I had that old, familiar feeling inside. I prepared myself for the final outcome. With a great peristaltic push to my alimentary canal, I opened my intestines to release what we all know, dear reader, as a silent-but-deadly. The luncheon of devilled kidneys and lamb's liver *Provençale* made a glorious, condensed, gaseous return and, once I had registered its heady perfume, I wound my scarf around my face. It was not long before that thin, sighing breathing of Mr. Merryweather was replaced with his muffled chokings of excruciating pain. He stared at me. Then, he glared at me! To finish off, I couldn't resist a hushed rebuke in his ear:

'That, my banking friend, will teach you to doubt my ethics and question our ability as detectives.' There was no reply, which was just as well, for at that moment, from my position peering over the cases in the direction of the floor, suddenly, my eyes caught the glint of a light.

At first it was a lurid spark upon the stone pavement. Then it lengthened out until it became a yellow line – enough to capture Merryweather's face in agony – and then, without any warning or sound, a gash of light. For a minute or more a hand, with its writhing fingers, protruded out of the floor. Then it was withdrawn as suddenly as it appeared, and all was dark again save the single lurid spark, which marked a chink between the stones.

Its disappearance, however, was momentary. With a rending, tearing sound, one of the broad, white stones turned over upon its side, and left a square, gaping hole, through which streamed the light of a lantern. Over the edge there peeped a clean-cut, boyish face, which looked keenly about it, and then, with a hand on either side of the aperture, drew itself shoulder high and waist high, until one knee rested upon the edge. In another instant he stood at the side of the hole, and was hauling after him a companion, lithe and small like himself and older, with a pale face, a beaky nose and a shock of ginger hair. The older man stood up. He was dressed immaculately in starched shirt and evening tails with a stethoscope around his neck. A nebula of cigarette smoke wafted into my nostrils and, sure enough, there was the tell-tale cigarette burning between his long, pale fingers. Once he had established his position, he looked around the space with his arms wavering around. When he spoke, any lingering doubts I had were dismissed on the first stutter.

'J..J...John! Arrrr yer shoo-wer that wee arrr inn the reet volt? I canna see no hair-no-high o'er the safes fer me to crrrr-ack open! W...what thi'divil is going on?'

So, we had a bank robber in the family. If Great Uncle Eric was to see me now, worse still to recognise me from that Christmas Day of many years ago, I wouldn't be able to shrug off the *sheer* and *utter* shame of it around London town. My reputation as a doctor would be ruined. One word from Mr. Merryweather and the banking community would blacklist me. Scotland

My Great Uncle Eric was a huge success in the City.
Now I knew why!

Yard would never forget the dismal association between the safe cracker and cracking safe detective's assistant. Worst of all, Holmes would be so embarrassed as the world's "greatest"private detective that he would be obliged to let our relationship lapse. This, therefore, was a personal disaster, if I allowed it to be thrust upon me, which I wouldn't. I took evasive action. I withdrew further back into the shadow of the cases and lay dead still. Now, I was no longer in a position to shoot the villains with my pistol and could hear only what was going on in the vault. When I considered this side effect, I resolved myself to inaction without responsibility because I remembered that it fired water only.

'The bullion is here all right,' said the boyish face. 'I did not spend five months planning and executing this operation only to break into the basement of the adjacent vegetarian restaurant. Ha, no! Nor would I have brought you into this plan if it wasn't for your safe-cracking superiority, you old ginger fogey, but it seems that Lady Luck is shining down upon us for it must be stored in those cases over there. Don't they make it easy for us to go about our business? But hold on, Eric? With no safes to crack, you have no use in this operation. Why do I need you any longer?'

I heard a splutter from my Great Uncle. I learned later on from my companions that he was responding to a gun being aimed at his heart by his more youthful companion in crime.

'Mebbe we have no need f' ma skeels with tha safes, ooer ma' stethoscope hee-yur, but you oonly have two arrrms by yoo-er sides, m'laddie, and yew'll need all the strrrrong arm help yer can git to moov tha boollion oot of this volt.'

'That is true,' he whispered. 'Now, it seems that the coast is all clear, so have you the chisel and the bags?'

'Aye, they'ur hee-yur!'

Suddenly, Sherlock Holmes sprung out and seized the young intruder by the collar.

'Great Scott! Jump, Eric! Jump, and I'll swing for it!'

I whipped my head round the side of the cases just in time to take in the rear view of Great Uncle Eric as he bolted towards the hole. Good! He was going to escape. But Jones suddenly leapt from the shadows and hurled himself at my withered relation. I heard the sound of rending cloth as the plod clutched at Eric's skirts, but it wasn't enough to stop him dropping down the hole and making his escape. That was fortunate!

But then I noticed the light flash upon the barrel of a revolver – not my own, dear reader, for mine was safely hidden away – but in the hand of the young criminal mastermind. Before he could pull the trigger, Holmes's hunting-crop came down on the man's wrist, and the pistol clinked upon the stone floor.

'It's no use, John Clay,' said Holmes blandly; 'you have no chance at all.'

'So, I see,'the other answered with the utmost coolness. 'I fancy that my pal is all right, though I see you have got his coat-tails.' Jones was holding up my uncle's coat tails in triumph.

'There are three men waiting for him by the door at the other end,' said Holmes.

'Oh, indeed? You seem to have done the thing very completely. I must compliment you.'

With Great Uncle Eric in the clink,
I could wave goodbye to my Christmas present!

'And I you,' Holmes answered. 'Your red-headed idea was very new and effective.'

'Ginger is the new blue,' said Clay, whatever that was supposed to mean.

'You'll see your pal again presently,' said Jones. 'He's quicker at climbing down holes than I am. Just hold out whilst I fix the darbies.'

'I beg that you will not touch me with your filthy hands!' remarked our prisoner, as the handcuffs clattered upon his wrists. 'You may not be aware that I have royal blood in my veins. Have the goodness also when you address me always to say "sir" and "please."'

'All right,' said Jones with a stare and a snigger. 'Well, would you please, sir, march upstairs, where we can get a cab to carry your highness to the police station.'

'That is better,' said John Clay, serenely. He made a sweeping bow to the three of us. 'Goodbye, Mr. Holmes. Until we meet again.' And he walked quietly off in the custody of the detective.

'Really, Mr. Holmes,' said Mr. Merryweather, as we followed them from the cellar, 'I do not know how the bank can thank you or repay you.'

'I do!' I said but was ignored.

'There is no doubt that you have detected and defeated in the most complete manner one of the most determined attempts at a bank robbery that ever come within my experience.'

'I have had one or two little scores to settle with Mr. John Clay,' said Holmes. 'I have been at some small expense over this matter, which I shall expect the bank to refund, but beyond that I am amply repaid by having had an experience which is in many ways unique, and by hearing the very remarkable narrative of the Red-headed League.'

And, once the great detective had declared his final position, he turned and walked towards the hansom that had been waiting for us. He shouted, 'Come along, Watson!' without breaking step or turning around. In that brief moment given to me, I was able to confront Mr. Merryweather and to thrust a note into his hand. The banker glanced reluctantly at the bill for one hundred and fifty pounds and made a small bow. 'It shall be delivered to you this evening. Well, to Mother Kelly's, precisely according to your instructions, Doctor.' We shook hands and I hurried along to join Holmes in the cab.

* * *

'You see, Watson,' he explained in the early hours of the morning, as we sat over a glass of whisky-and-soda in Mother Kelly's, 'it was perfectly obvious from the first that the only possible object of this rather fantastic business of the advertisement of the League, and the copying of the *Encyclopaedia*, must be to get this not over-bright ginger pawnbroker out of the way for a number of hours every day. It was a curious way of managing it, but really it would be difficult to suggest a better way. The method was no doubt suggested to Clay's ingenious mind by the colour of his accomplice's hair. The four pounds a week was a lure which must draw him, and what was it to them, who were playing for thousands. They put in the advertisement; one rogue has the temporary office, the other rogue incites the man to apply for it, and together they manage to secure his absence every morning in the week. From the time that I heard of the assistant having come for half wages, it was obvious to me that he had some strong motive for securing the situation.'

'But how could you guess what the motive was?'

'Had there been women in the house, I should have suspected a mere vulgar intrigue. That, however, was out of the question. The man's business was a small one, and there was nothing in his house which could account for such elaborate preparations and such an expenditure as they were at. It must then be something out of the house. What could it be? I thought of the assistant's fondness for photography, and his trick of vanishing into the cellar. The cellar! There was the end of this tangled clue. Then I made inquiries as to the mysterious assistant and found that I had to deal with one of the coolest and most daring criminals in London. He was doing something in the cellar – something which took many hours a day for months on end. Whatever could it be, once more? I could think of nothing save that he was running a tunnel to some other building.

'So far, I had got when we went to visit the scene of action. I surprised you by beating upon the pavement with my stick. I was ascertaining whether the cellar stretched out in front or behind. It was not in the front. Then I rang the bell, and, as I hoped, the assistant answered it. We have had some skirmishes, but we had never set eyes on each other before. I hardly looked at his face. His knees were what I wished to see. You must yourself have remarked how worn, wrinkled and stained they were. They spoke of those hours of burrowing. The only remaining point was what they were burrowing for. I walked around the corner, saw the City and Suburban Bank abutted on our friend's premises, and felt that I had solved my problem. Whilst you walked to your practice after the concert, I called upon Scotland Yard, and upon the chairman of the bank directors, with the result that you have seen.'

'And how could you tell that they would make their attempt tonight?' I asked.

'Well, when they closed their League offices that was a sign that they cared no longer about our Mr. Wilson; in other words, that they had completed their tunnel.'

'Good-bye Mr. Gingernuts!'

'Indeed, Watson. But it was essential that they should use the tunnel soon, as it might be discovered, or the bullion might be removed. Friday would suit them better than any other day, as it would give them two days for their escape. For all these reasons I expected them to come tonight.'

'You reasoned it out beautifully,' I exclaimed in unfeigned admiration. 'It is so long a chain, and yet every link rings true.'

'*And* it saved me from ennui,' he answered, yawning. 'My goodness I was getting terribly bored with life. Alas, I already feel it closing back in upon me! My life is spent in one long effort to escape from the commonplace of existence. These little problems help me to do so.'

'And you are a benefactor of the race,' said I.

'You are a sweety, darling.' He blew me a kiss.

'No, Holmes! You know that I mean what I say, from the heart.'

He shrugged his shoulders. 'Well, perhaps, after all, it is of some little use,' he remarked, and then he remembered something buried further back in his memory. 'Tell me, did you not wonder about the outcome of the flight of Clay's accomplice?'

'No, no, no Holmes,' I retorted, wishing for him to lose this line of conclusion as quickly as possible. 'In my opinion he was irrelevant, just a prawn in a sea of strategic intrigue. Besides, I hardly caught sight of him from my hiding place.'

'Did it not occur to you to maybe discover his identity? Did you not have a natural curiosity that begged for satisfaction?'

'No, no, no Holmes! What is the point? We have the master criminal behind bars, and I presume his accomplice resides with him.'

Holmes leaned back into his armchair. He closed his eyes and chuckled to himself. 'Ha! Indeed so, Watson. But whenever you deny a question thrice, I know that you are trying to hide something from me.'

No, no, n... Er, no, that is not always so, Holmes.'

He drummed his fingers in contemplation. 'Like the water pistol that you painted black to disguise it as an army revolver?'

I was struck speechless. He opened his eyes and smiled at my open dumbfoundedness. He laughed to himself again. Then, he looked over towards the girls. There sat three of the prettiest harlots in Mother Kelly's, all of them tall, feminine and athletic. Holmes leaned forwards towards me. He reached inside his top pocket, removed a scroll with his forefingers and handed it over. 'This, my good Doctor, is who our jailbird is.'

And, with that final revelation, Sherlock Holmes was finished. He stood up and ambled over to the girls, who were perched all-in-a-line upon the chaise longue. I unfurled the crisp paper scroll and the blood drained from my face. I had a terrible, sinking feeling as memories of Great Uncle Eric on Christmas Day 1847 swirled together with today's scenes from the City & Suburban bank vault. I was in a daze. What would Holmes think of me? Was this the end of our final adventure together? I watched him in his small talk with the harlots, pointing at himself and then over at me. When he was finished, he took the hand of the tall, sultry blonde and they walked towards the upstairs. Just before the first riser, he turned to look at me and said: 'Watson! For goodness sakes, stop moping and put that ten-shilling note to good use! "*Il faut manger ce qu'on chasse*!"

One should eat what one hunts? What the devil was he saying that for? And then a wave of relief washed over me and I laughed out loud as, would you believe it, dear reader, the prettiest of the three pullets sidled over and took me by the hand – a ginger-headed beauty with fiery red hair!